Walter Lantz®

A WOODY WOODPECKER BOOK

WOODY'S FIRST DICTIONARY

To: Matthew (7th Birthday

With Love:
    Dad + mom

By Deborah Kovacs • Illustrated by Eve Rose

PUBLISHERS • GROSSET & DUNLAP • NEW YORK

Aa

alligator
This **alligator** is angry.

alphabet
There are 26 letters in the **alphabet**.

a b c d e f
g h i j k l
m n o p q
r s t u v
w x y z

animals
Animals come in many shapes, sizes, and color.

apple
Sugarfoot's favorite food is a crunchy red **apple**.

Bb

ball
Charlie Beary likes to play **ball** with his son.

balloon
Oswald is holding one **balloon** too many.

bathroom
When Wally takes a bath, the **bathroom** gets very wet.

toothbrush

toothpaste

toilet

sink

towel

bathtub

soap

beach
On a warm day Winnie and Woody like to go to the **beach**.

water

sand

bear
A **bear** loves to eat honey.

bird
This **bird** is going south for the winter.

FLORIDA OR BUST

FLORIDA

bedroom
Andy Panda is sleeping in his **bedroom**.

closet

bed

pillow

nightstand

blanket

boat

Gabby Gator likes to fish from a **boat**.

body

Everyone has a **body**.

head

hand

arm

leg

foot

boy

Knothead is a **boy** bird.

bottle

Chilly Willy found a **bottle** with a message inside.

buzzard

A **buzzard** is a large bird that is sometimes mean.

box

A **box** sometimes holds a surprise.

To: Buzz
From: Woody

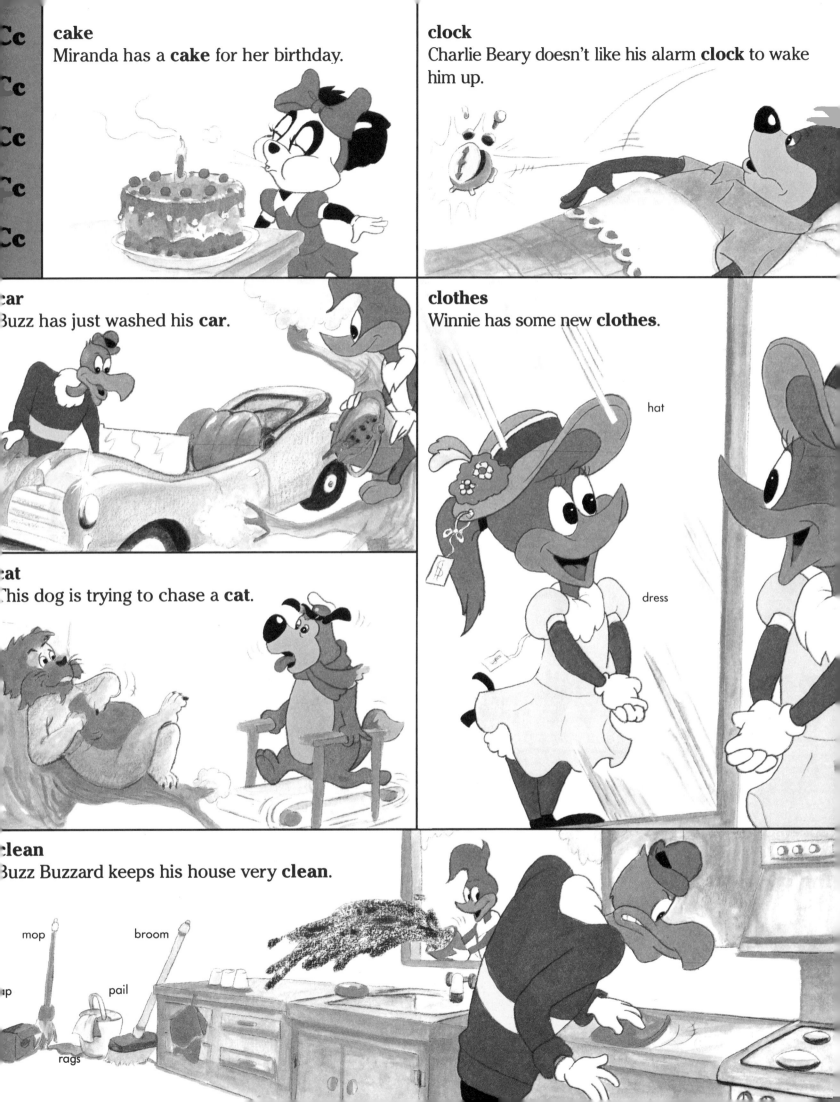

Cc

cake
Miranda has a **cake** for her birthday.

clock
Charlie Beary doesn't like his alarm **clock** to wake him up.

car
Buzz has just washed his **car**.

clothes
Winnie has some new **clothes**.

hat

dress

cat
This dog is trying to chase a **cat**.

clean
Buzz Buzzard keeps his house very **clean**.

mop

broom

pail

rags

cold
Chilly Willy lives in a very **cold** place.

cry
You **cry** when you are sad—and also when you slice onions.

colors
Can you find the seven **colors** in the rainbow?

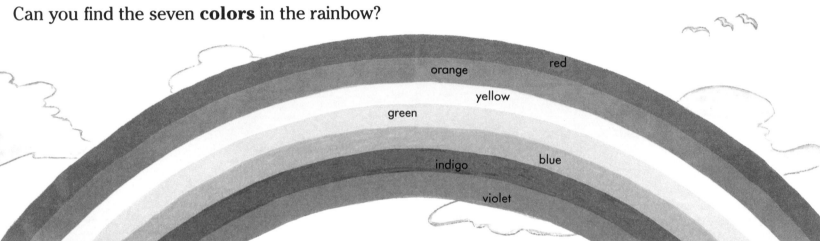

red
orange
yellow
green
blue
indigo
violet

Dd
Dd
Dd
Dd
Dd

dance
Andy and Miranda like to **dance**.

dog
A **dog** likes to dig up bones.

doctor
When Sugarfoot is sick, he goes to a horse **doctor**.

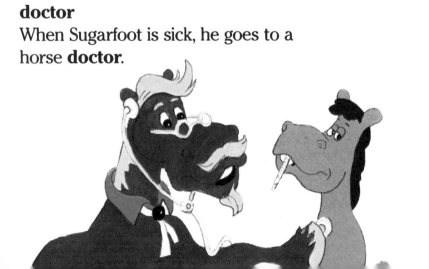

doll
Splinter is playing with her **doll**.

door
Woody is closing the **door** quickly.

down
Wally makes the seesaw go **down**.

Ee
Ee
Ee
Ee
Ee

Earth
Space Mouse can see our planet, **Earth**, from far away.

egg
Carrie has an **egg** in her nest.

eat
Smedly likes to **eat**.

elevator
An **elevator** is a machine that carries people and things up and down in a building.

escalator
An **escalator** is a set of moving stairs.

Ff
Ff
Ff
Ff
Ff

face
This is a funny **face**.

eyebrows
eyes
ear
nose
mouth

feather
Woody left a **feather** behind.

family
Here is a **family** of pandas.

father
mother
baby
brother
sister

fire fighter
A **fire fighter** puts out fires.

ladder
fire dog
truck
hose

farm
Oswald feeds the chickens on his **farm**.

horse
cow
pig
duck
goose
chicken

flower

ndy is giving Miranda a **flower** from his garden.

fruit

What do you get when you mix apples, oranges, pears, and bananas? **Fruit** salad!

fly

Woody can **fly** very fast.

game

Chilly Willy is playing a **game** of hide and seek with Smedly.

glasses

Glasses that protect the eyes from the sun are called sunglasses.

girl

plinter is a **girl** bird.

grass

Fresh green **grass** is one of Sugarfoot's favorite meals.

Hh
Hh
Hh
Hh
Hh

hat
Homer has a nice new straw **hat**.

hot
Gabby Gator lives in a **hot** place.

horse
Woody likes to ride his **horse**.

hug
Friends like to give each other a **hug**.

Ii
Ii
Ii
Ii
Ii

inside
Charlie Beary is **inside** his den.

Jj
Jj
Jj
Jj
Jj

juice
Gabby likes orange **juice**.

jump
A rabbit can **jump** far.

key
Buzz needs a **key** to start his car.

kitchen
Wally is making a snack in the **kitchen**.

cabinets

refrigerator

sink

counter

stove

iss
plinter sometimes gives Knothead a **kiss** on he cheek.

laugh
When Woody Woodpecker is happy, he laughs his special **laugh**.

HA HA HA
HA HA

aundry
hilly Willy is doing his **laundry**.

clothespin

thesline

detergent

basket

washer

dryer

letter
Homer Pigeon sent a **letter** to Carrie Pigeon.

light
When it is dark, you have to turn on a **light** to see.

library
There are lots of good books at the **library**.

living room
Woody and Winnie are sitting in the **living room**.

Mm

Mm

Mm

Mm

Mm

milk
Smedly likes to drink chocolate **milk**.

mirror
Wally looks in the **mirror** when he combs
his mustache.

oon
ace Mouse likes to
isit the **moon**.

mouse
A **mouse** likes to eat cheese.

nail
Gabby's vest is stuck on a **nail**.

noisy
When a paper bag pops, it is very **noisy**.

BOOM

apkin
harlie Beary uses a **napkin** to wipe his mouth.

numbers
We use **numbers** to count.

1
2
3
4
5
6
7
8
9
10

est
rrie Pigeon sleeps in a **nest**.

Oo

office
Gabby Gator is visiting the dentist's **office**.

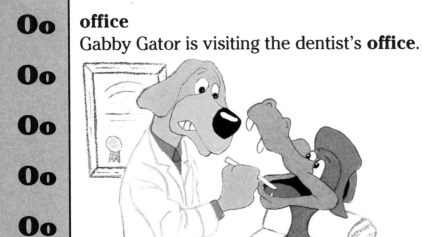

outside
Woody and Winnie are waiting **outside** the movie theater.

Pp

panda
A **panda** loves to eat bamboo.

pigeon
A **pigeon** is a bird that often lives in cities.

pencil
Woody is sharpening his last **pencil**.

penguin
A **penguin** is a bird without wings that lives in cold places.

playground
Knothead and Splinter have fun playing in the **playground**.

pocket
Chilly Willy fits nicely in Smedly's **pocket**.

puzzle
Buzz has almost finished his jigsaw **puzzle**.

Qq
Qq
Qq
Qq
Qq

quiet
"There's nothing like a little peace and **quiet**," says Woody.

Rr
Rr
Rr
Rr
Rr

rabbit
A **rabbit** has long ears.

rock
Oswald's burrow is under a **rock**.

radio
Woody and Winnie like to dance to music on the **radio**.

run
A horse can **run** fast…when it wants to.

Ss
Ss
Ss
Ss
Ss

sandwich
Wally likes to eat a **sandwich** for lunch.

snow
There is a lot of **snow** and ice near Chilly Willy's house.

snow

icicle

shovel

ice

snowflake

school
Smedly learned everything he knows at dog-training **school**.

chalkboard

HOW TO CATCH PENGUINS

teacher

scissors

paper

desk

crayons

paints

sock
Buzz has a hole in his **sock**.

shoe
Buzz wears one **shoe** on each foot.

steps
Andy Panda has to climb up the **steps** to see Miranda.

store
Space Mouse buys things for his spaceship at a special **store**.

space blanket

spacesuit

magazines

space food

books

street
Homer is very careful when he crosses the **street**.

stoplight

car

sidewalk

truck

sun
The **sun** shines and keeps us warm.

telephone
When they can't see each other, Winnie and Miranda talk on the **telephone**.

television
Have you ever seen Woody on **television**?

toys
Knothead has many different kinds of **toys**.

truck

shovel

top

car

pail

action figure

blocks

tree
Woody flew up a **tree**.

trick
Buzz enjoys playing a **trick** on Woody.

Uu

Uu

Uu

Uu

Uu

umbrella
An **umbrella** helps keep Miranda from getting wet in the rain.

up
Knothead is stuck **up** on the seesaw.

Vv

Vv

Vv

Vv

Vv

vacation
A **vacation** can be very relaxing.

vacuum cleaner
Woody's **vacuum cleaner** helps keep things tidy.

vegetables

Andy Panda likes to grow his own **vegetables**.

peas

carrots

lettuce

onions

corn

tomatoes

walk

Some animals **walk**, some run, and some fly.

wind

Sometimes the **wind** blows very hard where Wally lives.

walrus

Woody is giving Wally **Walrus** a drink of water.

wheel

Gabby's bicycle is missing a **wheel**.

woodpecker

A **woodpecker** finds his food by making holes in trees.

Ww
Ww
Ww
Ww
Ww

Xx

X ray
An **X ray** is a picture of the inside of your body.

xylophone
Wally plays beautiful music on his **xylophone**.

Yy

yard
Space Mouse likes to take care of his **yard**.

swing

garden

patio

lawn c

yo-yo
Knothead can do a lot of tricks with his **yo-yo**.

zoo
The **zoo** is home to many animals.

monkey

gira

Zz

zipper
Chilly Willy can't close the **zipper** on his jacket.

seal

lion

tiger